For Victoria and Alastair

First published in Great Britain in 2001 by Bloomsbury Publishing Plc
38 Soho Square, London, W1D 3HB

A CIP catalogue record of this book is available from the British Library
ISBN 0 7475 5056 5

Printed in Hong Kong by South China Printing Co.

1 3 5 7 9 10 8 6 4 2

Grandma's Beach

Rosalind Beardshaw

BLOOMSBURY
CHILDREN'S
BOOKS

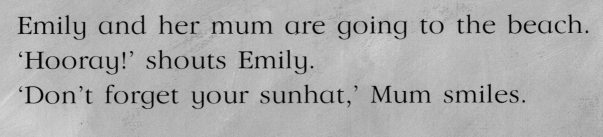

Emily and her mum are going to the beach.
'Hooray!' shouts Emily.
'Don't forget your sunhat,' Mum smiles.

As they packed the car,
Mum's phone rang.

'Hello? All right, I'll come to the office. But I'll have to take Emily to her grandma's first.'

But Grandma doesn't live at the seaside,
Emily thought sadly.

Emily's mum drove quickly to Grandma's house.
'Hello, Emily, what a lovely surprise,' said Gran.

'Hello, Grandma … I really wanted to go to the beach,' said Emily quietly.

'Well, go and put your beach things on and we'll see what we can do.'

'Bye, Emily. I'll pick you up later,' said Mum.

Whilst Emily was changing ...
Grandma got busy!

'Come on, Emily, everything's ready ...'

And when Emily came outside ...

'Quick – bring your fishing net to the rock pool, Emily.
I think I saw something.'

Then Grandma had another idea.
'Come on, Emily, let's build a sandcastle.'

'We'll see about that!' said Grandma.

'Watch out, Emily, the tide's coming in!'
'But, Grandma, there's no water!'
'That's what you think!'

'Let's sunbathe and dry off,' Grandma laughed.

Soon it was time for lunch.
'Fish and chips,' said Grandma.

'Mmmmm ... brilliant!' said
Emily, all covered in ketchup.

'Now close your eyes, Emily, I've got a surprise for you,' said Grandma.

'Look at you two!' said Mum as she came into the garden.
'I'm sorry we couldn't go to the beach today, Emily.
Shall we go tomorrow?'

'That's ok, Mum, I like Grandma's beach best!' said Emily.